Moroccan cuisine is considered among the oldest kitchens in the world, as it relies on spices in a way that makes the taste of Moroccan dishes prepared. In addition to the diversity of dishes, in this book I will show you how to prepare five of the father of Moroccan dishes

Moroccan tagine

One of the popular foods known in Morocco is the Moroccan tagine, which is one of the delicious and delicious foods, which is constantly present on the Moroccan trip and abounds in intent, and the tagine is a pot made of pottery, and what distinguishes it is that it is able to preserve the nutritional values of the cooked items in it, and also gives food A distinct flavor that does not appear in any kind of dishes prepared with regular pots, and the Moroccan tagine food is easy to prepare and its ingredients are available continuously, especially that the tagine can be made in more than one way and in different quantities, and we will present the method of Moroccan meat tagine and Mug chicken tagine my Lord.

Moroccan Meat Tagine

Ingredients

Kilograms of sliced meat. Onion, sliced. Two tomatoes. 2 cloves of garlic. Three tablespoons of vegetable oil. Five tablespoons of olive oil. Two hundred grams of carrots. One hundred grams of peas. Two potatoes. A cup of finely chopped fresh coriander. A teaspoon of ground ginger. A quarter of a teaspoon of saffron. Salt, to taste. The bowl for tagine cooking.

How to prepare

The pieces of meat are washed with cold water until red blood is removed. The aforementioned vegetables are washed on a vegetable cutting board and the carrots are cut into cubes. After peeling, the potatoes are cut into slices and the tomatoes into round slices as well. Place the pieces of meat in the tagine over medium heat with a little salt and bay leaf, and pour the water over the meat so that the pieces are slightly submerged, cover the tagine, and leave for a quarter of an hour. Add to the tagine slices of onions, potato slices, tomato slices, carrot pieces, peas, vegetable oil, olive oil, ginger, saffron, garlic, chopped coriander, and a little water, and leave the tagine for two hours. Casserole is served as it is on the dining table.

The Moroccan pastilla

Pastilla is a recipe from Moroccan cuisine and its preparation is spread widely in the Arab Maghreb, so the national dish is considered there, it is prepared with chicken, almond, or fish as desired and presented in Moroccan occasions such as weddings and banquets, and pastilla is the name of a very thin paper of dough called the paper pastilla, and it is called The name of the paper in Morocco, which is originally filo pastry or glash, during this article we will offer you an easy way to prepare pastilla with chicken.

The Pastilla

Ingredients :
500 grams large pastilla paper. Medium-sized chicken cleaned, washed and cut. A kilo and a half of chopped onion. 250 grams of almonds. Tablespoon of salt. A teaspoon of white pepper. Half a teaspoon of ginger. Two tablespoons of finely chopped cilantro. Two tablespoons of finely chopped parsley. A cup of vegetable oil. One and a half cup of melted butter. Ten eggs. 200 grams of fine sugar. Two tablespoons of ground cinnamon.

How to prepare :

We put the chicken in a bowl over the heat, then add the vegetable oil, stir the chicken pieces in the oil a little, then add the chopped onions. Add salt, pepper, saffron, ginger, butter, and stir together until well combined. Add the coriander and parsley and stir them, then add some boiling water to cover the chicken pieces completely. Cover the bowl and leave the chicken on the fire until done completely. Take the chicken pieces out of the broth, then set them aside to cool a little, and start by removing the bone from the chicken and cutting it into small pieces. We put the chicken broth over a boil until it thickens a little. Whisk the eggs slightly with a fork, then add them gradually over the broth, taking into account the rapid stirring. Transfer the almonds in the oil over the heat, then set aside to cool. We put the almonds in the food processor and grind it until it becomes very smooth, add 100 grams of sugar and 1 teaspoon of ground cinnamon and stir the mixture well. In the tray to be baked we put five sheets of pastilla so that the margins of the paper remain outside the tray, taking into account the greasing of each sheet with a thin layer of melted butter. We distribute a layer of chopped chicken, then put paper pastilla on top. Add a layer of chicken and egg broth, then put pastilla paper and finally distribute a layer of ground almond mixture and cover it with pastilla paper. Bend the notes of the pastilla leaf to the inside, then grease it with a layer of melted butter and put a final layer of pastilla paper so that it covers the last layer taking into account the fat being applied to the butter, and we can stick the paper with a beaten egg so that the paper does not open during roasting. We put the tray in the oven until browned and golden. It can be decorated with honey, chopped almonds, or with ground sugar and cinnamon.

The Moroccan seffa

The Moroccan seffa is a dish that does not include any Moroccan table or feast, and your guests in the evening or in an intimate tea session must have a dish from the Moroccan seffa, whether it is a regular, couscous or buried noodles, all you need to provide a distinct and elegant fit for the guests

How to prepare the Moroccan seffa

Ingredients:

1Kg lattice is very thin, especially with the sword

100 grams raisins without bone

100 gr butter

200 g boiled, peeled and fried almonds in oil and crushed

1 tablespoon of cinnamon for garnish

250 grams fine satin sugar
salt

4 tablespoons vegetable oil

How to prepare a seffa

We put the thin noodles in a large bowl and mind them with two tablespoons of oil.
Fill half of the couscous pot with water, then put it over a moderate heat.
When the water boils, put in a thin, oiled, fried noodles in oil to cook steamed.
Boil two liters of water.
After about 15 minutes of steamed cooking, pour the boiled water over the noodles.
Let it drip well.
And then we mind the noodles with oil the amount of 2 tablespoons and let it cool slightly.
Then put it in the couscous again and put it on steamed again for 15 minutes.
We repeat the same process again (steps 4, 5, 6, 7, 8).
Then we drizzle the noodles well from the water
Put it in a large pot and add a little salt
Then we add: 150 g of fine sugar and raisins and mix all well
Then we return the cuff to evaporate for the last time for 10 minutes.
And then we put the cuff in a bowl, then add butter and mix them well.
 Place the dish on the serving plate, and garnish with cinnamon, sugar, my dress, and ground almonds.
Rebekah offers small plates of fine sugar.

the Moroccan HARIRA

Moroccan HARIRA
It is a kind of soup
Famous in Morocco, and the Moroccan HARIRA is usually presented in the month of Ramadan. The Harira dish is an integrated medicine in terms of food. It is full of healthy components that are beneficial to the body, especially in the month of Ramadan. Its components differ from one region to another, and we will present it today according to the original Moroccan method.

Quantities

1 cup shred meat
1 cup chickpeas
2 medium onions
2 medium tomatoes
2 tablespoons of butter
2 tablespoons of vermicelli
2 tablespoons of flour
2 tablespoons of tomato Lord
1 1/2 liter water
1/2 teaspoon saffron
1 teaspoon salt
1 teaspoon black pepper
2 tablespoons of coriander
2 tablespoons of parsley

How to prepare HARIRA

1- We put the chickpeas in a bowl, immerse them in water and leave it for the next day

2- We cut the onions into small pieces and put them in a large saucepan with a little butter and salt over medium heat until the onion is withered

3- We add the meat to the onion and black pepper and stir it to change its color then add only a liter of water and leave it on the heat for about 20 minutes

4- After making sure that the meat is done, add the hummus after filtering it from the water

5- Mash the tomatoes in the mixer until they become sauce, then add it to the meat and chickpeas mixture, saffron saffron and stir well.

6- In a pint of remaining water, we dissolve the flour and tomato Lord and add them to the mixture while stirring constantly until the mixture thickens

7- We add the coriander and noodles to the calories and leave them on low heat for five minutes until the noodles are done

8- Pour the calories into small pots and decorate them with parsley, and they are ready to be served.

The Moroccan BISARA

The Moroccan BISARA

It is a popular Moroccan food consisting of beans and peas and can be prepared in the winter because it gives the body energy and warmth, is easy to prepare and rich in vitamins and minerals.

Ingredients OF Bisara:

1/2 kilo crushed, washed, ground beans

1/2 kilo crushed, washed peas

2 large onions, finely chopped

1/2 cup parsley, washed and chopped fine

1/2 cup soft washed and chopped coriander

Salt / pepper to taste

5 large garlic cloves

Water for cooking

4 tablespoons of cumin

4 tablespoons olive oil

How to prepare

1- In a bowl, put all the beans, peas, onions, garlic, parsley, green coriander and water to put on the heat.
2- Leave to boil, lower the temperature of the fire, cover and leave for an hour with continuous monitoring and stirring.
3- We can add water if it is dry.
4- Then remove from the heat and leave to cool a little and mix with the electric mixer and then filtered with a filter and put it back in the bowl again.
5- Put on heat, season with salt and pepper, and leave for 7 minutes.
6- Remove from heat, add cumin and olive oil, and serve.

Next book dishes

chebbakya

msemen

baghrir

loubya

kaab ghzal

THANK YOU